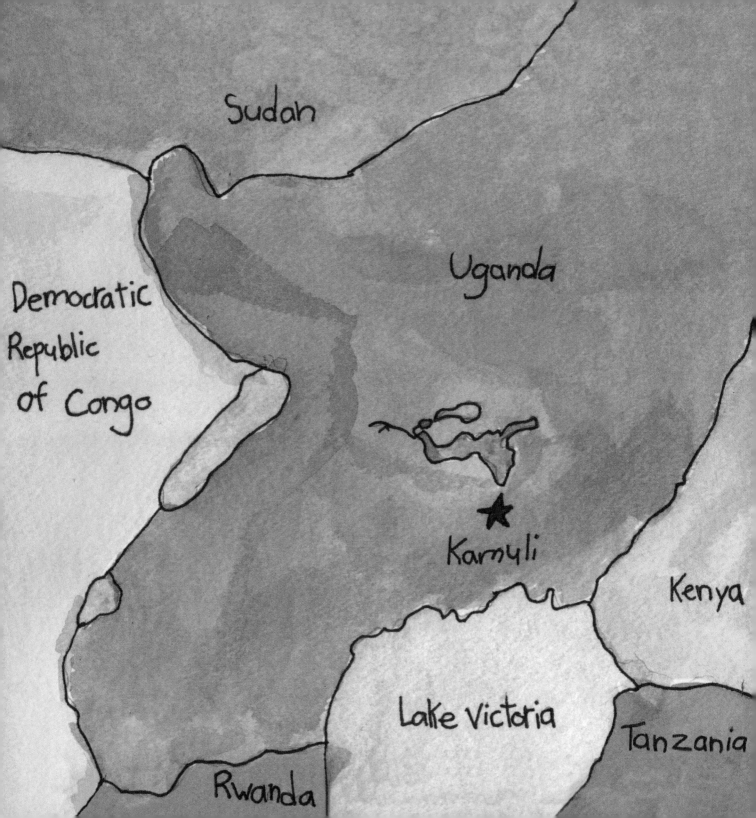

About the Author

Teagan Read is eight years old and lives in Vancouver, Canada. She is an avid artist and is passionate about writing. This book, her first publication, was inspired by a news article about a team traveling to Uganda to build a well in an impoverished village. When Teagan heard that 350 children lived in the village and didn't have a clean supply of drinking water, she immediately wanted to help. She decided to write and illustrate this book to raise funds to help build wells in Kamuli, Uganda and in other areas of Africa.

Kya's Treasure

Written and illustrated by
Teagan Read

This book is dedicated to all of the children in Uganda.

May you find all of your treasures.

Once there was a girl named Kya. She lived in a small
village called Kamuli in Uganda. She was named after the
stars because she was born during a beautiful clear night.
She loved her name because it meant "diamond in the sky"
and reminded her of sparkling jewels.

One hot and sunny day Kya had nothing to do so she decided to go look for treasure. She was excited because nobody had ever done that before in her village.

She started walking along a gravelly path and came to a magnificent crocodile.

"What are you looking for?" asked the crocodile.
"I'm looking for a treasure !" Kya answered.
"I have just the treasure you want," he replied.

"This is a very nice doll, but it's not the treasure I'm looking for," said Kya.

Kya started walking on the path again.
She went down a long hill and at the bottom she
saw a tall tree with a giraffe standing near it.

"What are you looking for?" asked the giraffe.
"A treasure," answered Kya.

"Well I have a spectacular treasure for you!" exclaimed
the giraffe. "Look in my tree!"

Kya followed the giraffe and saw three golden leaves dangling off a branch.

"Those are fabulous golden leaves but it's not the treasure I'm looking for," she said.

"Well, have a good time looking for your treasure," replied the giraffe, secretly relieved that Kya didn't take the leaves.

Kya continued on her way. Soon the gravelly path became dirty. The dirt turned into mud. In a mud puddle on the side of the path Kya spotted a young hippopotamus.

"What are you looking for?" asked the hippo.

"A treasure," said Kya. "A treasure that glistens in the sun."

"I think you will like the treasure that I have," replied the hippo.
"Come with me and I will show you."

The hippo showed Kya a beautiful silver coin that glistened in the sun.

"That does glisten in the sun, but it's not what I'm looking for," Kya said.

Kya continued on the muddy path. Soon it was dry again and tall grasses appeared. Suddenly an antelope bounced over to her through the grass.

"What are you looking for?" asked the antelope.
"A treasure," said Kya. "A treasure that is so **COOL** ."

The antelope led Kya through the tall grass to a shiny red car.
"This is the coolest car ever!" he said.

"That is definitely a cool car," Kya said, "but it's not the cool treasure I'm looking for."

Starting to feel sad, hot and tired, Kya continued on her journey. She soon found a rock and sat down to rest. Suddenly she felt the ground start to shake. She looked up and saw an elephant stomping over.

"What's the matter?" asked the elephant.
"I'm looking for a treasure," said Kya. " A treasure that can *drip* and sometimes you can see *ripples* in it."

"Ohhh. I know the perfect treasure that can drip and has ripples in it," said the elephant.

Kya followed the elephant, hoping that this would be the end of her journey, but it wasn't what she was looking for. It was a large, melting chocolate fudge ice cream cone!

"Sorry, that's not the treasure I'm looking for, but it sure looks delicious!" exclaimed Kya.

Kya felt that she should go home. Would she ever find the treasure? She decided to look in one more place over by the next hill. Just when she thought she couldn't take another step.....

she looked up and finally found her

SPECIAL

glistening

COOLING

dripping

rippling

treasure!

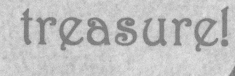

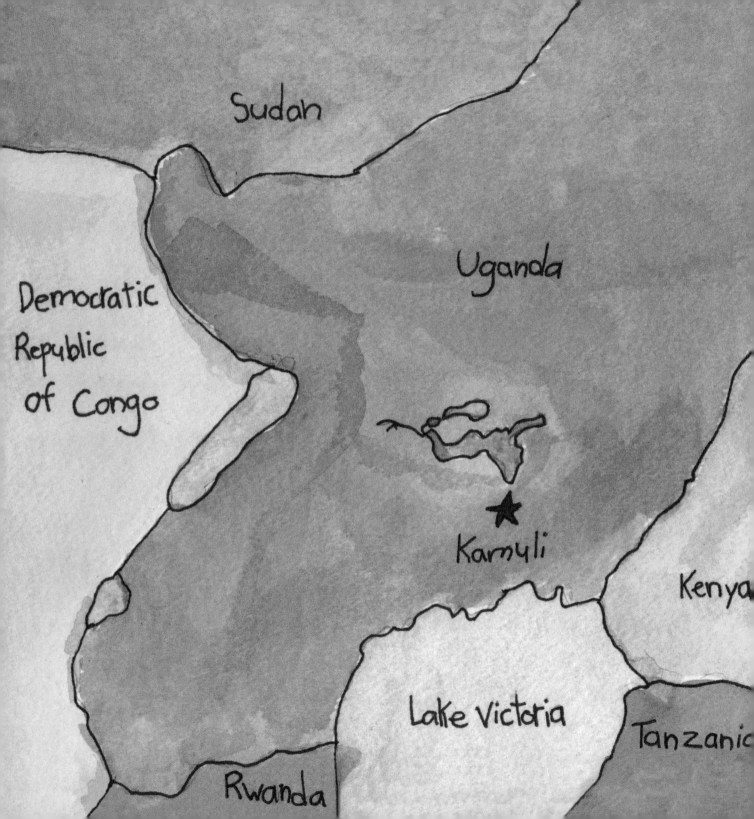

Made in the USA
Charleston, SC
25 October 2013